ONCE UPON A TiM

BOOK I

STUART GIBBS

ILLUSTRATED BY STACY CURTIS

SIMON & SCHUSTER BOOKS FOR YOUNG READERS

NEW YORK LONDON TORONTO SYDNEY NEW DELHI

For Violet and Dashiell—S. G.

For Carol Carpenter—S. C.

SIMON & SCHUSTER BOOKS FOR YOUNG READERS

An imprint of Simon & Schuster Children's Publishing Division

1230 Avenue of the Americas, New York, New York 10020

SIMON & SCHUSTER BOOKS FOR YOUNG READERS

and related marks are trademarks of Simon & Schuster, Inc.

For information about special discounts for bulk purchases, please contact Simon & Schuster Special Sales at 1-866-506-1949 or business@simonandschuster.com.

The Simon & Schuster Speakers Bureau can bring authors to your live event. For more information or to book an event, contact the Simon & Schuster Speakers Bureau at 1-866-248-3049 or visit our website at www.simonspeakers.com.

The text for this book was set in Adobe Caslon Pro.

Manufactured in the United States of America

0723 BVG

4 6 8 10 9 7 5 3

Library of Congress Cataloging-in-Publication Data

Names: Gibbs, Stuart, 1969– author. | Curtis, Stacy, illustrator.

Title: Once upon a Tim / Stuart Gibbs ; [illustrated by] Stacy Curtis.

Description: First Simon & Schuster Books for Young Readers hardcover edition. | New York : Simon & Schuster Books for Young Readers, 2022. | Audience: Ages 7–10. | Audience: Grades 2–3. | Summary: With no knightly experience but plenty of pluck and an impressive vocabulary, a twelve-year-old peasant, hoping to improve his station in life, volunteers to help a cowardly prince and his not very powerful wizard rescue a princess from an evil, foul-smelling monster.

Identifiers: LCCN 2021016381 (print) | LCCN 2021016382 (ebook) | ISBN 9781534499256 (board) | ISBN 9781534499270 (ebook)

Subjects: CYAC: Knights and knighthood—Fiction. | Peasants—Fiction. | Adventure and adventurers—Fiction. | Humorous stories. | LCGFT: Novels. | Humorous fiction.

Classification: LCC PZ7.G339236 On 2022 (print) | LCC PZ7.G339236 (ebook) | DDC [Fic]—dc23

LC record available at https://lccn.loc.gov/2021016381

LC ebook record available at https://lccn.loc.gov/2021016382

CHAPTER ONE

Who I Am

ONCE UPON A TIME...

There was a prince who was revered throughout the land for being exceptionally brave...

who was known far and wide for his cool and calm presence in the face of grave danger . . .

and who was beloved and adored by all the people of his kingdom.

This is not his story.

It's mine.

I'm Tim.

Come in a little closer so you can have a better look at me.

You know how, whenever you see a movie or read a story set in olden times, it's almost always about a dashing prince or a beautiful princess, and you're supposed to get all wrapped up in their troubles?

Well, there are *lots* of other people who aren't princes or princesses, and trust me: we have way more problems than the rich folks do.

We're called peasants. And being a peasant *stinks*.

To start with, we're all really, really poor.

See those clothes I'm wearing? *Those are the only clothes*

I own. I've been wearing the same outfit for two years—and it was a hand-me-down from a cousin who wore it for two years before *me.*

All the princes and princesses live in castles with hundreds of rooms. I live in a *hut.*

See?

You might be thinking to yourself, *Gosh, that's awfully small, but it looks pretty cozy.*

Well, it's not. For example, look at the windows....

Oh, that's right. You can't. *Because there aren't any windows.* Peasants can't afford fancy stuff like glass. Which means that any animal that wants to get into your house can do it: flies, lice, raccoons, muskrats, wild boars, the occasional dragon . . .

While I'm on the subject, here are a few other things we don't have:

Air-conditioning.

Heaters.

Refrigerators.

Televisions.

Internet.

Bathrooms.

Yes, you heard that right. We don't have bathrooms. No showers. No sinks. No *toilets.* (All right, I'll admit, the princes and princesses don't have flush toilets either, but they at least have separate rooms to do their business and professional wipers to clean them afterward.)

But the worst part of being a peasant isn't really what we don't have.

It's what we can't *do*.

See, there's only one way to become a prince or princess: you're born into it. That's it. No one can apply for a job as a royal family member. If you're a peasant boy, like me, you basically have one option:

TIM'S FAMILY TREE

TIM

My parents are peasants. So were their parents. And their parents before them. And so on and so on and so on, going all the way back as far as anyone can remember. (Which, given that there aren't any history books readily available, is about seventy years.) There's nothing you can do about it.

Almost.

It turns out, there *is* one way a peasant can change his lot in life. It isn't easy, though. In fact, it's extremely dangerous. Ridiculously, terribly, insanely dangerous. But if you're smart, brave, confident, trustworthy, honest—and if you don't die in the process—then you might be able to pull it off.

I was willing to give it a shot.

Because, like I said, being a peasant stinks. (Okay, I'll admit, some people are content with peasantry. Like my parents. And all my uncles and aunts. And all my distant cousins. And most of my neighbors. But it just wasn't for me.)

So . . . this is the story of how I took that shot. And how it led to the greatest adventure of my young life—along with plenty of danger and peril and treachery and doom.

It's a good story, though. I promise. And there are some awesome pictures, too. So settle down, get cozy, maybe make a quick stop to use the bathroom (with your flush toilet, you lucky duck), and I'll tell it to you.

Right now.

CHAPTER TWO

What Started It All

Even though this is *my* story, it begins with a princess. This princess, right here:

This is Princess Grace, who lives in the next kingdom over from me. Before this adventure, I had never met her, so I only knew as much about her as you do from looking at this picture. She was famous for being beautiful and lovely and kind. People said that she had a voice like an angel, and that when she sang, woodland creatures would gather around and gaze at her adoringly, although you can't really believe everything you hear. But she did have quite a good reputation. . . .

And then *this* happened.

Princess Grace was snatched away by a monster. And not just any monster. The most horrible, terrible, deadly monster you can imagine.

No, not a dragon. Dragons are powder puffs compared to what I'm talking about.

She was taken by a stinx.

Not a sphinx. A stinx.

A sphinx is a creature with the head of a human, the body of a lion, the wings of a bat, and a habit of asking really terrible riddles.

A stinx is far worse.

It has the left side of a lion, the wings of a bat, and the right side of an entirely different lion who doesn't get along with the first, so it is always in an incredibly bad mood.

Also, as you might have gathered from its name, it smells awful. Worse than awful, really. It has the most toxic, terrible, malodorous stench of anything you have ever encountered. ⬆ IQ BOOSTER!

(I recognize that you might not know what "malodorous" means. Occasionally I'm going to drop a big word in here and then share the definition. That way, if your parents ever start giving you grief for reading a book with lots of pictures in it, you can tell them it's actually educational. Then wow them with one of the words you've learned. They'll be so impressed, they might even let you stay up past your bedtime to keep reading. For help finding them, I'll even throw in those handy IQ Booster arrows.)

Anyhow, "malodorous" means "really, really, *really* smelly." Imagine the smelliest thing you can think of, and then triple it. The kind of smelly that could kill a canary. (If your parents challenge you to use the word in a sentence, say "Whenever Mom passes gas, it's extremely *malodorous*." That ought to end the conversation right there.)

So, a stinx has two heads that don't get along, which makes it very little fun to hang out with, and a smell that keeps anyone from coming within five miles of it. Therefore, they are the most ill-tempered, vile, and nasty creatures that ever lived and are prone to doing jerky things like capturing princesses, knocking over churches, and urinating in the town reservoir.

Of course, everyone in the kingdom was extremely upset that their princess had been captured. Especially her parents.

But the king and queen also saw an opportunity here. If you've ever read a fairy tale, you know that the standard way for a princess to meet a prince is to end up in peril. The princess gets captured by a vicious beast, or moves in with a bunch of dwarfs and then eats a poisoned apple— or, if she's a real drama-queen-to-be, she pricks her finger on a spinning wheel and falls asleep for a hundred years along with the rest of her kingdom. Then the prince comes along and rescues her, they immediately fall in love, and all is well and good.

(I know, I know. It would probably be much more efficient if they just had social mixers, but that's the way things were done back in my day.)

So the call went out to all the nearby kingdoms to see if there were any dashing, daring, and eligible young princes who wanted to rescue the princess and win her hand in marriage.

Since my kingdom happened to be right next door, we were the first to hear about the situation with the stinx. And our prince was very intrigued.

Remember that prince I mentioned before? The one at the beginning of the book? Here's another picture of him to jog your memory:

This is Prince Ruprecht. He'd always had a serious crush on Princess Grace. And his parents, King and Queen Goodheart (who are right behind him) liked Grace a lot too. But not because she was beautiful or smart or strangely attractive to woodland creatures. It was because she was *rich*.

You see, King and Queen Goodheart might have ruled our kingdom and lived in a really big castle with 164 rooms and personal buttocks wipers, but they weren't very smart. As a result, they made some really bad investments. Recently, they had blown their entire fortune on a goose that was supposed to lay golden eggs. (It turned out to be just a regular goose. It could have at least made a nice meal—except that the king then traded it for some "magic beans," which, of course, turned out to just be regular beans and were promptly eaten by a mouse.)

Anyhow, Prince Ruprecht decided to answer the call, defeat the stinx, rescue the princess, and win her hand in marriage (along with all her money).

There were just two problems:

1) Ruprecht was a coward.

I know that, back in chapter 1, I made it sound like he

was very brave. But if you read that section again, you'll notice something: I only said that he was *revered* for being brave. That doesn't mean he was *actually* brave. It just means he had really good public relations.

All the people of my kingdom had been tricked by this. Including me. As you will see, I would eventually learn the truth about Ruprecht the hard way.

2) Ruprecht didn't have any knights to join him on his quest. Once our knights had learned that the king and queen had blown all their money on a goose, they went to work for royals who could actually afford to pay them.

Having no knights and no courage left Ruprecht in a bit of a pickle.

But then his sinister adviser, Nerlim, came up with a plan.

Nerlim was a sneaky, shifty guy— and royals always need sneaky and shifty people to advise them. Nerlim was the one who had spread all the rumors that Ruprecht was brave and dashing in the first place. And he'd also covered up the story of the bad goose investment.

Now he came to Prince Ruprecht with a plan that was quite dastardly. **IQ BOOSTER!** (Did you notice I dropped another good word in there? "Dastardly" means "wicked," "cruel," or "really, really, jerky." As in: "The dastardly school administrator cut the budget for new books for the library.")

The plan was also clever and devious. But it required someone they could take advantage of. Someone well meaning and dutiful and trustworthy who they could trick.

Basically, it required a sucker.

Sadly, that's where I come in.

CHAPTER THREE

How I Got Suckered

I was chopping wood with my best friend, Belinda, when I first heard about the princess.

It was around noon on a day in spring. I'm not sure *what* day, exactly, because we didn't have months. Or days of the week. There were rumors that in some distant land, people were working on a calendar, trying to figure out how many months there should be in a year and how many days there should be in a week and arguing about what to name them, but I didn't think too much about it. When you do the exact same thing every day, day in and day out, it doesn't really matter what the day is *named*, does it?

If I'd owned a calendar, it would have just looked like this:

I suspect you're thinking one of two things:

1) Wow. That looks terrible.

2) Wow! That looks amazing! You don't have any school!

If you're in the second group, let me tell you something: if someone had given me the chance to go sit in a room filled with other kids my age and learn about amazing things like math and science for several hours a day instead of staying at home and doing chores, I would have dropped to my knees and kissed their feet. I am not saying this because your local Parent-Teacher Association bribed me to. I am saying this because it's true. Maybe you like school. Or maybe you think it's the worst thing ever. But if you think it's the worst thing ever, *you're totally, completely, entirely wrong.*

There are many, many, many worse things than school. For example: work. Which is what I had to do all day, every day. Chopping wood. Harvesting crops. Hauling water from the well. Picking lice out of my parents' hair. All of that is difficult, exhausting, and no fun at all. (Although for that matter, I hear that being a professional royal-buttocks wiper is even worse.)

Here's another thing that's a lot worse than school: Facing off against vicious, bloodthirsty monsters. Doing that is no picnic, as you'll soon find out. . . .

But I'm getting ahead of myself.

The point is, I was chopping wood with Belinda when we heard the news. Belinda was not supposed to be chopping wood at all, because she was a girl, although both of us thought that was ridiculous. In our time, girls were only supposed to do stereotypical girly things like making dinner, scrubbing floors, taking care of children, and, if they were princesses, getting abducted by mythical creatures. If they had calendars, they'd look like this:

Each cell of the calendar reads:
Dawn: Wake up
Paylight hours: Stereotypical girly things.
Night: Sleep.

The final cell reads:
Dawn: Wake up
Paylight hours: Get abducted by basilisk
Night: Pass out in fear.

However, Belinda's calendar wouldn't look like that, because she was an iconoclast. IQ BOOSTER!

(An iconoclast is someone who rebels against the usual way of thinking. Like, in my time, there were some icono-clasts who insisted that the earth wasn't actually the center of the universe, with the sun and the moon and every-thing else revolving around it, and that, in fact, the earth revolved around the sun. We thought all those folks were even nuttier than the people who believed you could repel dragons by putting broccoli in your shoes.)

For the record, iconoclasts often don't get treated very well. Lots of folks are afraid of people who think differently than they do—and that was the case with Belinda.

While I was annoyed by my lack of options in life, Belinda's options were even worse. If a girl wasn't born royal, she had two career choices: housewife or witch. Belinda hated the idea of being a housewife, and she didn't have the skills to be a witch. She was terrible at casting spells. Almost every time she tried to put a spell on something, it didn't work. Nothing would happen at all. (Although once, she managed to turn a carrot into a rutabaga—but it still tasted awfully carroty afterward.)

Belinda was not supposed to be chopping wood with me that day. She was supposed to be mending her father's best (and only) pair of knickers. But she had snuck out to help me instead. We were in the woods near the castle, felling an oak tree, when the town crier came along.

That day, he was crying a lot more than usual.

The official job of the town crier was to deliver important news, and sadly, just about all the news we ever got was terrible. Cattle disease. Goat disease. Rat infestations. Infestations of diseased rats. Marauding orcs. (And that was all in the same day.) So the town crier was always very upset. In fact, we could usually tell how bad the news was just by his style of crying. A soft whimper signaled news that was only mildly distressing, like our town's wheat supply getting moldy, whereas heavy weeping indicated something far worse, like a dragon eating one of the townsfolk. But I had never heard him cry like he was doing that day.

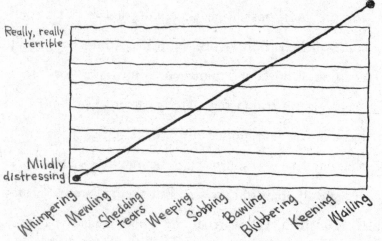

Neither Belinda nor I had ever heard the crier like this before. We stopped our chopping.

"What happened?" Belinda asked.

The crier was wailing so badly, he could barely get the words out between fits of sobs. "Princess . . . WAAAAAHHHH . . . Grace . . . AAAAUUGGHH . . . has . . . BOOHOOHOOHOO . . . been . . . AAAAA-AAA . . . taken."

I dropped my ax in surprise. "Taken where? And by what?"

The crier was too upset to answer. He burst into tears again, then blew his nose loudly into a soggy handkerchief that had obviously been used way too many times that day.

Belinda and I shared a look of concern. Neither of us knew Princess Grace, of course. I had only seen her once, when her royal processional passed my town, and even then I only caught a glimpse of her hair through the window of her carriage from a quarter mile away. But since she was famous for being kind and sweet and strangely appealing to woodland creatures, the idea that anything bad had happened to her was very upsetting to Belinda and me. *IQ BOOSTER!*

The crier continued weeping so copiously that he had

to sit down. ("Copiously" means "in large quantities." As in: "Anyone who drinks water copiously will have to pee fifty times a day.") Unable to talk, he fished a royal decree from his tunic and handed it to me.

I unrolled the parchment. This is what it said:

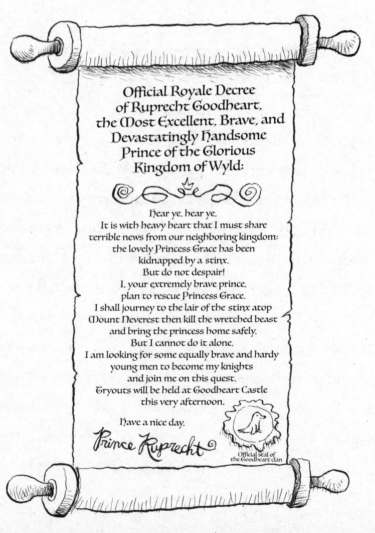

Official Royale Decree
of Ruprecht Goodheart,
the Most Excellent, Brave, and
Devastatingly Handsome
Prince of the Glorious
Kingdom of Wyld:

Hear ye, hear ye,
It is with heavy heart that I must share
terrible news from our neighboring kingdom:
the lovely Princess Grace has been
kidnapped by a stinx.
But do not despair!
I, your extremely brave prince,
plan to rescue Princess Grace.
I shall journey to the lair of the stinx atop
Mount Neverest then kill the wretched beast
and bring the princess home safely.
But I cannot do it alone.
I am looking for some equally brave and hardy
young men to become my knights
and join me on this quest.
Tryouts will be held at Goodheart Castle
this very afternoon.

Have a nice day,

Prince Ruprecht

Official seal of
the Goodheart clan

Upon reading this, I experienced two very different emotions.

I was very sad to hear about Princess Grace.

But, I hate to admit, deep down inside, I was also kind of excited.

There had never been a call to recruit knights in the Kingdom of Wyld before.

Remember, back at the end of chapter 1, when I told you there was a way that a peasant could change his life? Well, this was it.

You didn't need to come from a noble background to be a knight. You didn't need to be of royal birth. You didn't need to be rich. All you needed to be was brave, courageous, plucky, fearless, adventurous, determined, and willing to look death in the eye on a regular basis.

And in this particular case, you also needed to be gullible. Although I didn't know that at the time.

("Gullible" means that you can be easily tricked. For example, tell your best friend that if they look up "gullible" in the dictionary, they will find a photo of themselves. If they do it, then they are gullible—and you will have a nice laugh at their expense.)

The trick that Ruprecht and Nerlim were playing, however, was not quite as good-natured. The truth was, they weren't really looking for knights at all. They were looking for people who they could fool into *thinking* that they were knights. Gullible people.

Like me.

"I'm going to do this," I said.

And to my surprise, Belinda said, "Me too!"

CHAPTER FOUR

Why Belinda Came Along

"You *can't* become a knight," I told Belinda. "Knights are boys. And you're a girl."

"I'm well aware of that," she replied. "Which is why I'm not going to *tell* anyone that I'm a girl."

We were hurrying through town toward Goodheart Castle, figuring that the tryouts for becoming a knight would be starting soon. Prince Ruprecht hadn't given a specific time for the tryouts, but that made sense, because no one ever really knew what time it was anyhow. The day was divided up like this:

Dawn

Daytime

Dusk

Night

CASTLE

TOWN
WELL

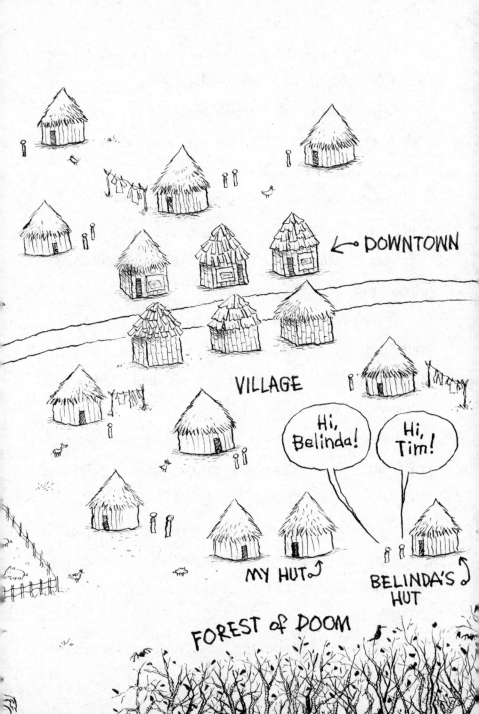

We didn't have hours or minutes or seconds. Things just sort of happened when they happened.

Even though I didn't know exactly *when* the tryouts would be taking place, I didn't want to miss them.

And neither did Belinda.

Both of us were walking as fast as we could.

I said, "I think they're going to notice you're a girl, whether we tell them or not. You have a ponytail. And a dress. And, er . . . girl parts."

"That's not a problem," Belinda said confidently. "It's not hard to look like a boy. All I have to do is tuck my ponytail up under my hat, steal some boy's clothes, and then act dumber than usual."

"Ha-ha," I said. "You won't be laughing when they see right through your disguise and realize you're a girl. Then they'll be angry with you."

"They're not going to see through my disguise. Because *you're* going to help me fool them. You're going to say that I'm your cousin from a faraway kingdom."

"But I don't *want* to do that."

Belinda stopped walking through the center of town

and gave me a hard stare. "Why not? Are you afraid you'll get in trouble?"

"No," I said. "I'm just, well . . . afraid."

"Afraid?"

"Being a knight is dangerous! And you're only a girl!"

"You're only a boy! Isn't it going to be dangerous for you, too?"

"Yes. But this is my one shot to escape the peasantry."

"It's my one shot too." Belinda's hard stare softened, and I saw that it wasn't *me* she was angry at. It was everything else. "Tim, if you think *you* have a lousy lot in life, how do you think *I* feel? You might hate being a peasant, but at least you have the option to try to become a knight. I don't even have that. I'll be stuck being a bored housewife or a lousy witch. Which means that I'll be miserable for the rest of my life. Unless you help convince Prince Ruprecht that I'm a boy."

I thought about this for a good long while. Knights were supposed to be trustworthy, and lying to everyone about Belinda seemed like a crummy thing to do.

But then, not helping my friend seemed even crummier. Plus, now that I thought about it, the rule that knights had to be men was ridiculous. Belinda was smarter and braver than anyone else I knew. If I was going on a dangerous quest, I couldn't imagine anyone better to have by my side. (Well, technically, I suppose it would have been nice to have a giant with the strength of a hundred men or a well-trained dragon by my side. But as far as *humans* were concerned, Belinda was my number one pick.)

"Okay," I agreed finally. "I'll do it."

A huge grin spread across Belinda's face. "You will? You're the best friend ever!"

"But I really don't think it's going to work," I said.

"Yes it will. Watch!"

We happened to be standing in front of her cousins' house—which really wasn't a big coincidence, as our town wasn't huge, and almost everyone was related to everyone else. (My own cousins' house was right next door, and my second cousins were right next to that.)

Belinda's cousin Humphrey was about her age, and his freshly washed clothes were drying on the line. Belinda quickly "borrowed" them, then ducked behind the house and changed.

When she came back, I have to admit, I was surprised. She looked more like a boy than I had expected. Her usual patches of dirt and tattered pants really helped sell it.

And so we headed off to the knight tryouts at the castle . . .

Only to be stunned by what we discovered there.

CHAPTER FIVE

How I Became a Knight

When we arrived at the castle, the tryouts looked like this:

Belinda and I were the only ones who had shown up. Except for our village idiot, Ferkle, who had just wandered in by accident because he was looking for some mud to put in his pants.

Therefore, Prince Ruprecht looked like *this*:

He was apoplectic ⟨ IQ BOOSTER!] that his tryouts were so poorly attended, as he felt it meant that his subjects didn't like him very much.

("Apoplectic" means "really, really angry." As in: "My mother was apoplectic after I said that her farts were malodorous.")

In truth, there were probably lots of reasons why people hadn't shown up. Most of the peasants in the village were very busy, doing things like hunting or farming so that their families wouldn't starve to death. And there were probably lots of people who didn't want to be Ruprecht's knights because they weren't that brave, or they were too old, or they were allergic to stinx dander.

Although it's quite likely that everyone else in town simply wasn't as gullible as Belinda and me.

Since the whole knight-tryout thing was Nerlim's idea, he was *very* excited to see us arrive. He hurried over and greeted us with great enthusiasm.

"Well, hello!" he said, speaking in a voice loud enough for Ruprecht to hear. "It's a pleasure to see two such strapping and brave young men answering the call of duty to become knights!" Then he thought of something and asked us quietly, "Er . . . you *are* here for the tryouts, yes? Not to put mud in your pants?"

"No," I said. "We're here to be knights."

Nerlim heaved a sigh of relief. Then he resumed his loud voice for Ruprecht again. "Very good! Are you subjects of the prince?"

"Yes," I said. "I live on the edge of town. My name's Tim. And this is Bel . . ."

Oops. I almost gave everything away, right off the bat. I caught myself, but it was too late.

"Belle?" Nerlim asked, suspicious.

"*Bull*," Belinda said in a gruff voice. "I'm Tim's cousin,

from a few kingdoms over. I'm on a boar-hunting trip,
but when I heard there were knight tryouts, I jumped at
the chance. I'm not the kind of guy who leaves a damsel
in distress." She then spit on the ground and
scratched her butt.

I had to admit, she looked the part. In fact, she seemed
to be acting like a better boy than *me*. So I spit and
scratched my butt too.

Nerlim smiled, pleased. "I like your attitude, young

man! So then, are both of you prepared to take the test for knighthood?"

"Yes!" I said, although it might not have come off quite as enthusiastic as I had hoped, because I was a little bit worried about what the test might entail.

I had been so wrapped up in the idea of becoming a knight to escape my humdrum life that I had forgotten all about the fact that I didn't have any skills to speak of. Being a peasant, I'd had no training for knighthood. I could wield an ax but had never even held a sword. I had milked a cow but never ridden a horse. And I had never faced off against a vicious creature like a dragon or a stinx. The most dangerous beast I had ever confronted was a raccoon that was trying to steal my underwear off the clothesline.

So now I was a bit worried. I glanced over at Belinda, thinking that she might be equally unsettled, but she appeared quite calm and confident.

"Very good!" Nerlim said. "Let's begin! Are both of you willing to swear allegiance to Prince Ruprecht?"

"Yes!" Belinda and I said.

"Are you willing to go on this quest to rescue Princess Grace from the vile and vicious stinx?"

"Yes!"

"Will you follow the orders of your leader without hesitation?"

"Yes!"

"Congratulations!" Nerlim said. "You passed!"

I shared a confused glance with Belinda. "We did?"

"Yes!" Nerlim exclaimed. "With flying colors!"

"Er . . . ," Belinda said. "Don't you want to see if we can ride horses? Or joust? Or wield a sword? Or . . . anything?"

"Not really," Nerlim replied. "We must get this rescue mission underway as quickly as possible. So we don't have time for a whole lot of jousting and stabbing and gouging. Besides, the most important thing a knight needs is blind devotion to the cause."

"Not skill with a sword?" Belinda asked.

"Oh, sure, that comes in handy," Nerlim said quickly. "But superb sword skills don't mean a thing if the knight is a scaredy-cat who runs away from battle. Both of you seem very enthusiastic. I think you're exactly what we want on this force. Welcome aboard!" He called out to Prince Ruprecht. "These two young men are going to join our quest!"

"Sounds good," Ruprecht said, though not nearly as heartily as I would have expected. He then pointed to Ferkle, who now had several buckets' worth of mud in his pants. "Let's take that guy too, while we're at it."

"Him?" Belinda cried. "That's the village idiot! He's wearing a live chicken instead of a hat! He can't possibly be a knight!"

Nerlim shrugged. "He showed up for the tryouts. That shows gumption."

Belinda started to protest again, but I cut her off. I didn't care that our test hadn't been difficult. In fact, I was *thrilled*. We had been selected as knights! So what if the process seemed a little sketchy?

"Thank you," I told Nerlim. "We are very excited to be part of the force. What do we do next?"

"Go home and pack your bags," Nerlim said. "Then report back here at first light. Tomorrow, we embark on our glorious quest to face the stinx!"

Even though this was frightening, I was still ecstatic. And despite her concerns, Belinda appeared excited as well. With only a few questions, our fates had changed course. We were no longer mere peasants, stuck doing the same, boring thing day after day for the rest of our lives. We were going on a quest! We would get to leave our little village for the first time! We would get to face horribly dangerous creatures that would try to kill us!

Actually, that last sentence probably shouldn't have had an exclamation point, but that's how happy I was. I was so desperate to stop being a peasant, I was willing to face the occasional stinx.

Although, as it turned out, I really should have been more worried about Nerlim and Ruprecht.

CHAPTER SIX

How My Parents Felt about All This

My parents weren't as happy about me becoming a knight as I had hoped.

Not because they were concerned for my safety. To be honest, being a peasant was rather treacherous. Peasants routinely got kicked in the head by mules, or lost limbs in plowing accidents, or were devoured by marauding dragons. Only two days before, one of the peasants who lived down the lane had accidentally stepped on a leprechaun while herding his goats, and the little jerk had put a pox on him that turned him turquoise and made his ears swell to the size of dinner plates.

What really bothered my parents was that they, like so many people, were afraid of change.

"What's wrong with being a peasant?" my mother asked at supper that night.

"*Everything,*" I replied. "It's boring, it's hard, it's dangerous, it's filthy, it's exhausting, it doesn't pay well, there's no dental plan . . ."

"But *we're* peasants," my father said, sounding slightly offended. "And so were our parents. And their parents. And their parents before them. All your uncles and aunts are peasants. And your cousins. And, well . . . pretty much every other person we know. Except for the royals. If it's good enough for all of us, why isn't it good enough for you?"

I sighed. "I just want something *more.*"

"More than this?" Mom asked, surprised, waving a hand around our hut.

I considered our home, checking out our mud walls, our dirt floor, our glassless windows, the piles of flea-ridden thatch we used for beds, our wobbly table and chairs, our hand-me-down kettle, the gruel we were having for dinner, the rat making off with a crust of bread, and the clouds of flies and mosquitoes that were always hovering around.

"Er . . . yes," I said. "I want *much* more than this."

My father said, "You realize, when you're a knight, you will have to leave our village and travel to strange places?"

"I am fine with that," I said. "In fact, I find it *exciting*."

My mother said, "You might have to eat things that aren't gruel."

"Mom," I said, "don't take this the wrong way, but I'm kind of sick of gruel."

My parents both looked shocked.

I realize that, maybe, you don't know what gruel is. Here's my mother's recipe, which had been handed down for generations:

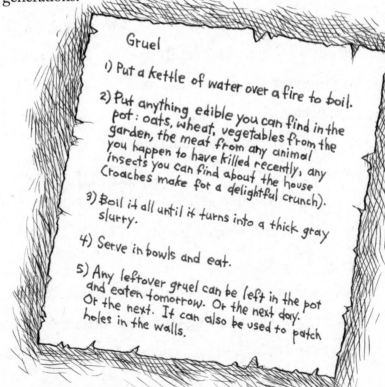

Gruel

1) Put a kettle of water over a fire to boil.

2) Put anything edible you can find in the pot: oats, wheat, vegetables from the garden, the meat from any animal you happen to have killed recently, any insects you can find about the house (roaches make for a delightful crunch).

3) Boil it all until it turns into a thick gray slurry.

4) Serve in bowls and eat.

5) Any leftover gruel can be left in the pot and eaten tomorrow. Or the next day. Or the next. It can also be used to patch holes in the walls.

"How could you be sick of gruel?" my father asked.

"Well . . . ," I said, "we've eaten it three meals a day for my entire life."

"If you want a change, I could mix things up," my mother told me. "How about, if tomorrow for lunch, instead of gruel, we have gruel sandwiches?"

"Er . . . ," I said, "don't we usually eat gruel and bread?"

"Yes," my mother replied enthusiastically. "But this time, I could put the gruel *on* the bread!"

"Whoa now," my father said, looking uneasy. "Let's not get crazy here. Our family has been eating gruel *near* bread forever. Gruel *on* bread sounds as though it might be dangerous."

As you can probably tell from this conversation, my parents are very provincial. ◁ IQ BOOSTER! ("Provincial" means "narrow-minded and unsophisticated.") My parents weren't this way on purpose. They just hadn't seen much of the world.

"I appreciate the offer to change things," I told my mother. "But I'm not going to be here tomorrow. I'm going with the other knights on a quest to save Princess Grace."

My parents tried repeatedly to talk me out of this, but my mind was made up. Eventually, they realized they weren't going to change that. So they gave me their blessing and wished me well, but it was obvious that they weren't happy.

I wondered if I should have just done what Belinda was doing with her parents. After careful consideration, she had decided that the best way to handle the situation was to lie to them. She told them that she was going away to witch school to get a degree in advanced sorcery. They were thrilled.

I set to work, packing my things for my journey the next day, which didn't take long, as I didn't own very much. For example, I didn't have to pack any spare clothes, because I didn't have any.

Then I took some time to say goodbye to my faithful fr-dog, Rover.

That's not a typo. I don't have a dog. I have a fr-dog. He *used* to be a dog, but he kept digging up the vegetable garden of our next-door neighbor, Witch Waydideego. One day, Witch Waydideego got fed up and turned him into a frog. Sort of. She wasn't a very good witch, so Rover ended up as a large frog that acts exactly like a dog. A fr-dog.

He's still a great pet, though. He is loyal and loving, although he's a bit slimy. And now, when he chases squirrels, he can actually catch them.

Eventually, my father came over, looking sad.

"I don't really understand why you want to be a knight," he said, "but I hope you find what you're looking for."

"You mean, a sense of purpose in my life?" I asked.

"Er . . . no," Dad said, looking confused. "I meant the stinx. That's what you're looking for, right? So you can rescue Princess Grace?"

"Oh," I said. "Yes. That's the purpose of the quest. Thanks."

"I just hope you know what you're doing," my father said.

"I do," I assured him.

But I really didn't. Not at all.

CHAPTER SEVEN

Why the Quest Got Off to a Bad Start

As promised, Belinda and I reported to Goodheart Castle first thing in the morning, ready to begin our quest.

Nerlim met us there, as did Ferkle, although it turned out that was no big deal, as Ferkle hadn't even gone home. He'd gotten his head stuck in one of the castle's cannons and spent the night there.

Prince Ruprecht was late.

Even though we were at *his* castle, we still had to wait for him. It turned out, princes normally don't get up at the crack of dawn. They do something called "sleeping in," which is where you lie in a "bed" until you feel like getting up, which, according to Nerlim, could be sometime in the middle of the day for Ruprecht.

Apparently princes don't have chores.

Nerlim had roused him, but Prince Ruprecht was groggy and cantankerous ⟨ IQ BOOSTER! ⟩ and took his sweet time getting dressed and ready. ("Cantankerous" means "bad-tempered." As in: "The cantankerous librarian kept shushing me every time I laughed at the hilarious book I was reading.")

While we waited for Ruprecht, Nerlim took care of outfitting us with everything we needed to be knights.

He took us to the armory to get swords and knives and crossbows.

He took us to the forge to get armor.

He took us to the stables to get horses and saddles.

And then, because Ruprecht *still* wasn't ready, we practiced with our weapons for a bit on the castle artillery range.

I had some skill with a crossbow and a knife, as I had hunted for food a lot, and while it took me a while to get the hang of a sword, I was in good physical shape after all my days working the fields and chopping wood. So I wasn't too bad with my weapons.

Belinda had a bit more trouble, because, as a girl, she had less opportunity to hunt or work the fields. (She wasn't supposed to do either of those things at all, but occasionally she snuck away from her knitting or sweeping to join me.) She wasn't particularly accurate with a weapon, but she was definitely enthusiastic.

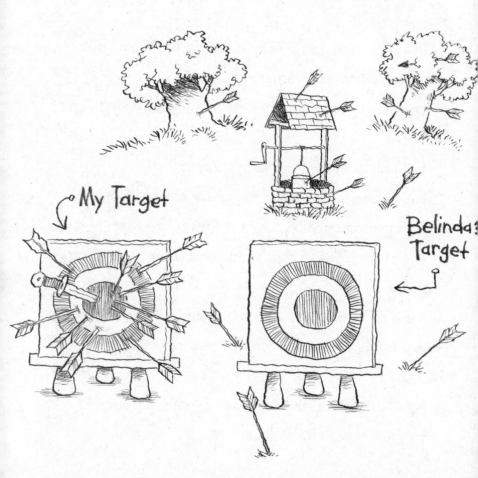

Meanwhile, Ferkle somehow got the hilt of his knife stuck up his nose.

Right now you might be wondering to yourself, *Why do you even have a village idiot?*

The answer is: I don't know.

Our village had had an idiot for as long as anyone could remember. So did every other village. Ferkle's father had been an idiot, and his father before him, and his father before him. They didn't really do much or contribute to the town in any way, but every now and then, they were good for a laugh. (I understand that such people even exist in your time, although they are no longer called village idiots. They are called television talk show hosts.)

By the time Ruprecht finally showed up (still grumpy because he hadn't had a full night's sleep), we were completely outfitted, somewhat trained, and raring to go. So we hopped onto our horses and began our quest.

You may have noticed that Belinda and I didn't look quite as impressive as Ruprecht.

As prince, Ruprecht got a lot of things that we didn't. Like a custom-made, form-fitting suit of armor. Which was nice and shiny, because it had never been worn. And he had his own horse, a gallant steed named Charger, while Belinda and I got some old horses that were well past their prime. (Of course, we still looked more impressive than Ferkle, but, then, I've seen foot fungus that looks more impressive than Ferkle.)

However, no one was really looking at us anyhow. They were all looking at Ruprecht.

The whole town came out to see us off, as it was big news that a quest had been launched to save Princess Grace. Everyone lined the street (not the streets; we only had one road in town) and cheered for Ruprecht as he bravely led the way. Any grogginess or cantankerousness he had shown at the castle vanished as we made our way through the village. He smiled brightly and waved to the townsfolk, pausing every now and then to wink at a young woman, who would promptly swoon. ⟨ IQ BOOSTER! ⟩

(To swoon is to faint from extreme emotion. It seems

kind of ridiculous that this is something we would even
need a word for, but it happened quite a lot when Ruprecht
was around. Women—and the occasional man—swooned
left and right as he passed by. After we were done,
the street was piled with swooned bodies.)

However, once we were outside town and away from the townspeople, Prince Ruprecht stopped smiling and winking. He grew grumpy and sullen again.

"How much farther is it?" he asked Nerlim.

"Er . . . it's quite a long way," Nerlim replied. "We're still within sight of the village."

"Ugh," Ruprecht said with a groan. "This is booooor-ing. When are we going to get there?"

"Not for a long while," Nerlim said, looking quite irritated.

"Can't you just do some magic and get us there instantly?" Ruprecht asked.

Nerlim stopped looking irritated and began looking embarrassed. "Um . . . no."

"Why not?" Ruprecht whined.

"Because I said so. That's why."

I shared a look with Belinda. We had always been told that Nerlim was a great and powerful wizard. But now it occurred to me that the person who had told us that was Nerlim himself. He was always proclaiming things like, "Behold! I am Nerlim, the great and powerful wizard! Do

not cross me, or I shall turn you into a newt!" However,
I had never seen him turn anyone into a newt. Or any
type of amphibian, for that matter. And his answer to
Ruprecht's question seemed really evasive. ◁ IQ BOOSTER !

("Evasive" means that it sounded like Nerlim was
avoiding the question, as though he didn't have a good
answer for it. Adults are often evasive when answering
perfectly good questions that kids ask, like "Why are
you allowed to use bad words when I can't?" "Where do
babies come from?" and "Can I get a new dog because
my old one got turned into a frog?")

Given Belinda's look, she seemed to be suspicious of
Nerlim as well.

I glanced at Ferkle. He didn't seem suspicious at all.
Instead, he was busily trying to eat one of his shoes.

Ruprecht didn't seem suspicious either. He was sulky
and moody. His bad mood had returned with a vengeance.
"Where is this lousy stinx's lair anyway?" he groused.

"I'm glad you asked!" Nerlim cried, seeming relieved
that he could change the subject. "I have a map right here!"

He pulled a roll of parchment from his robe and unfurled

it for us. We gathered around to take a look. (Except for Ferkle, who was distracted by a very pretty butterfly.)

I felt a shiver go up my spine.

"Wow," I said. "There's an awful lot of doom in our kingdom."

"Yes," Belinda agreed. "Plus, whoever named all these places wasn't very creative."

I asked Nerlim, "How far is it to the Forest of Doom?"

"I don't think it's too far," Nerlim replied.

At which point Ferkle gave a bloodcurdling scream of abject terror.

We all looked up from the map again. Nerlim's face went pale with fear.

"In fact," he said, "I think we're there."

CHAPTER EIGHT

How We Survived the First Monster

We're going to start this chapter with an IQ Booster and talk about something called "perspective."

How something looks depends on where you are viewing it from. So something that is very far away will look very small. Like the Mountains of Doom. We could see them in the distance, but they looked very tiny and innocent, like baby teeth, even though they were quite big and jagged and dangerous, like fangs.

Remember that butterfly I mentioned near the end of the last chapter? The one that Ferkle had been looking at? Well, at the time, I had been distracted by the map, so I wasn't paying much attention. I *thought* that it was a small, innocent butterfly that was relatively nearby.

But that was a trick of perspective. What we were actually seeing was an incredibly large, extremely dangerous,
bloodthirsty Butterfly of Doom from a long distance away.

While we had been looking at the map, it had come
much closer, and now it looked like this:

This was a bit of a surprise.

I admit, I had been hoping to get a lot farther into our journey without running into any monsters. But if we *did* run into monsters, I had been expecting that they would look, well . . . less butterfly-like.

Still, this one was trying to steal Ferkle, so Belinda and I quickly unsheathed our swords and tried to fend it off.

This didn't go so well. Even though the butterfly was big, it could move quickly; every time we tried to stab it, it flitted out of the way. Plus, butterflies are insects, so they have six legs. That meant this vicious Butterfly of Doom could clutch Ferkle in two of its legs and fight off Belinda and me with the other four. Meanwhile, each flap of its enormous wings created great gusts of wind that nearly knocked us off our feet.

Oh, and also, I wasn't used to fighting in armor. Armor is *heavy*. So it wasn't long before Belinda and I were exhausted from our repeated (but failed) attempts to stab the butterfly. Then the vicious beast knocked our swords from our hands and blew us down with a mighty flap of its beautiful wings.

We were powerless to stop it. It gave a high-pitched squeak (turns out, Butterflies of Doom don't roar) and was about to fly off with Ferkle when . . .

Rover, my fr-dog, had come to our rescue! I had left him at home, thinking that pets wouldn't be allowed on royal quests, but it appeared that he, being faithful and loyal, had followed me. Then, upon seeing that I was in grave danger, he had rushed to save me. (Or maybe he was just hungry.)

Whatever the case, he quickly gulped the butterfly down, then gave a satisfied belch.

Ferkle lay on the ground, gibbering fearfully.

And then, to my surprise, Nerlim turned on Rover. "A giant Toad of Doom!" he yelped. "Kill it! Kill it! Kill it!"

I leapt in front of Rover to protect him. "This isn't a Toad of Doom! It's my fr-dog, Rover!"

Nerlim gave Rover and me a wary glance. "This horrid beast belongs to you?"

"Yes. And he's not horrid. He's loyal and true . . ."

Rover gave me a friendly lick with his great big tongue, leaving a trail of slobber and giant butterfly guts on my cheek.

". . . although he is a bit slimy," I finished.

"I'm not going on a quest with something that disgusting!" Prince Ruprecht announced, hopping out from behind a tree, quite a distance away from us. "Send him home right now!"

At the harsh tone of Ruprecht's voice, Rover made sad puppy fr-dog eyes at me and whimpered.

"We can't send Rover home," Belinda said. "He just saved Ferkle's life! Instead of running away and hiding behind a tree, like some princes I could mention."

"I didn't run away!" Ruprecht said defensively. "And I

wasn't hiding! I thought I heard *another* giant butterfly behind that tree. A bigger and meaner one! So I went over there to slay it!"

"Sure you did," said Belinda.

"I *did*," Ruprecht insisted. "I'm the Most Excellent and Brave Prince Ruprecht! I laugh at danger! I'm not afraid of some silly butterfl—YIKES!!! THERE'S ANOTHER ONE!!!"

Sure enough, another giant, evil butterfly was coming for us. But before it could . . .

After this, Nerlim changed his attitude. "Hmmmm," he said thoughtfully. "I suppose this beast, however disgusting, *could* be of aid to us on our journey. Don't you agree, Ruprecht?" He looked around for the prince, confused. "Ruprecht?"

"I'm right over here!" Ruprecht announced, stepping out from a tree that was even farther away than the first one. "Looking for, er ... other giant butterflies that I could kill. Certainly not hiding. Nope. Not me!"

Belinda and I shared another look. It was quickly becoming evident to us that Brave Prince Ruprecht might not be so brave after all.

And when you combined that with the fact that Nerlim's magical powers seemed to be questionable—*and* the fact that we had barely made it out of the village before almost losing one of our fellow knights to a butterfly— it began to seem as though our quest didn't have much chance of succeeding. I was sorely tempted to suggest that we all give up and turn back.

But I didn't. For a few reasons:

First, Princess Grace's life was still in grave danger. And *someone* had to save her.

Second, going back would mean giving up on my

dreams. If I quit being a knight, then I might never get another chance. I would be stuck as a peasant for the rest of my life, always wondering what might have happened if I hadn't given up.

Third, we had Rover with us now. And while he wasn't a knight, he had at least proven to be very good at killing Butterflies of Doom.

So instead, I gave Rover a pat on the head, told him "Good fr-dog," then hopped back on my horse and looked at the others. "We're wasting time," I said. "Are we going to rescue the princess or not?"

Until I said this, Prince Ruprecht had looked as though he would have been happy to turn around and head home and perhaps spend the rest of the day in bed. But now he wasn't about to do that, because then I would look braver than he was. So he puffed out his chest and proclaimed, "Let's go, fellow knights! The princess isn't going to rescue herself!"

Everyone got back onto their horses, and we headed into the Forest of Doom.

CHAPTER NINE

How We Made It through the Forest of Doom

In my whole life, I had never ventured very far beyond my village. Now, as we headed deeper and deeper into the Forest of Doom, I began to think that staying home had been an extremely wise decision. The forest was awfully spooky. The trees were so tall and dense that it felt like night, even in the middle of the day. There were shadows everywhere, and I had the sense that something big and mean was lurking in each and every one of them, waiting for a chance to attack us. Weird, scary noises echoed throughout. It was all quite unsettling.

Ferkle, who had nearly been killed once already that day, was shaking so badly that his armor rattled like a bag full of tin cans.

I think Ruprecht might have been shaking too, but his armor fit a lot better, so it was harder to tell.

However, Rover was as happy as I had ever seen him. Dogs (and fr-dogs) really love three things: walks, weird smells, and food. So this was fr-dog paradise. We were on a very long walk, everything in the forest smelled strange—and there was plenty to eat. Every time a giant bug attacked us (which happened quite a lot) . . . ZAP! Rover would flick his giant tongue, and the next thing you knew, the insect was gone.

ZAP! There went a king-sized cockroach.

ZAP! So much for that colossal dung beetle.

ZAP! ZAP! ZAP! Goodbye, massive mosquito. So long, giant spider. Bye-bye, big old bedbug.

Things kept coming at us, and Rover kept devouring them. Gargantuan ◀ IQ BOOSTER! ▶ grasshoppers. Elephantine ◀ IQ BOOSTER! ▶ earwigs. Brobdingnagian bees. (All those words I just used mean "really, really big.")

Rover protected us over and over and over again, although, by the time we reached the far edge of the forest, he looked like this:

I think if he had tried to eat one more bug, he would have barfed.

He was *very* happy, though. If he still had a tail, he would have been wagging it wildly.

We were happy too, because we had survived the Forest of Doom.

Now all we had to do was make it over the River of Doom, the Chasm of Doom, and the Mountains of Doom.

"Rats," I said.

"What's wrong?" Belinda asked.

"I was hoping that we'd at least have a brief break before encountering something doom-y," I told her. "Like maybe, the Fields of Joy. Or the Path of Pleasantness. I'd even be all right with a Swamp of Mediocrity."

"This river doesn't look so bad," Belinda said.

I considered the river. She was right.

It looked like this:

It was calm and serene. There were no scary creatures lurking on the banks or ominous ⟨IQ BOOSTER!⟩ dorsal fins slicing through the surface.

("Ominous" means "giving the impression that something bad is about to happen." For example, when I tell you that things are going to get very bad by the end of this chapter, I am being ominous.)

"This looks way better than 'not so bad'!" Prince Ruprecht proclaimed. "It looks pretty darn great! And look! There's even a raft!"

Sure enough, there was a large, sturdy raft right at the riverbank.

"I get to be in the front!" Ruprecht exclaimed, spurring his horse toward it.

"Wait, Your Excellency!" Nerlim exclaimed, moving his own horse into Ruprecht's path and forcing him to stop. "There's something suspicious about all this."

"Suspicious?" Ruprecht repeated mockingly. "Nerlim, stop being such a scaredy-cat. Everything here looks perfectly fine!"

"*That's* what I'm afraid of," Nerlim said. "This *is* called the River of Doom. Why would it be called the River of Doom if there wasn't any doom?"

"Maybe it was a marketing thing," Ruprecht said. "Like when the Vikings discovered Iceland and Greenland, and Iceland was nice, while Greenland sucked eggs, but the Vikings didn't want anyone else to know that, so they called the icy island Greenland to trick people into going there and called the green island Iceland so that everyone would avoid it. My uncle, King Snodgrass, did the exact same thing. He discovered a beautiful place to build a kingdom, but he didn't want anyone invading him, so he named it Plague City, and now everyone avoids it like, well, the plague."

"Plague City is actually nice?" Nerlim asked, surprised. "I'd heard that place was a cesspit."

"Exactly!" Ruprecht said. "It's all marketing! So let's get going! This river looks fabulous!"

With that, he rode his horse onto the raft.

The rest of us followed him. Because, despite Nerlim's words of caution, the river really did seem surprisingly peaceful and non-threatening. (Of course, a battlefield would have seemed peaceful and non-threatening after the Forest of Doom.) Then we shoved away from the riverbank and calmly floated downstream.

The sun was shining. The river was beautiful. No ridiculously large insects were trying to kill us. It was all quite pleasant.

For a short while.

As you may recall, we didn't measure time using minutes. So I'd say the pleasantness lasted about the length of time it took to make a nice gruel sandwich.

And then things went very bad, very fast.

CHAPTER TEN

Why I No Longer Like Traveling on Rivers

The first sign that something was wrong was a very loud borborygmus.  SUPER IQ BOOSTER!

(The reason I threw that "SUPER" in there is that I'm going to bet that even your parents don't know this word, although they should. A borborygmus is the weird gurgling noise your stomach makes sometimes. The plural is borborygmi. I know, it sounds like I am making this up, but I am not. It's a real word. Go look it up if you don't believe me.)

I figured the borborygmus was coming from Belinda. So I looked over to her. "Are you hungry?"

"Not really," she said. "Watching Rover eat all those bugs made me kind of nauseated. Why do you ask?"

"I thought I heard your stomach grumble."

She shook her head. "I thought that was *your* stomach."

I looked to the others on the raft. They all seemed too far away for me to have heard a borborygmus from them.

So then I figured, maybe, it was from one of the horses. Or Rover. If anyone's stomach should have been making funny noises, it was my fr-dog's.

Now I noticed that the horses and Rover were all looking skittish. As if they were beginning to seriously regret coming on the raft. Like this:

Which made *me* skittish.

And if that wasn't bad enough, I noticed another sound. The sound of rushing water.

The river was beginning to pick up speed. We were now moving downstream rather quickly toward a series of dangerous rapids and whirlpools, which lay not far ahead.

And then I heard another borborygmus. It was much louder this time. Loud enough for everyone on the raft to hear.

In fact, it was so loud, the whole raft trembled.

"My goodness," Nerlim said. "One of you must be *really* hungry."

The horses and Rover were now *extremely* skittish.

"Um . . . ," I said worriedly. "I don't think that was one of our stomachs. Or the horses'. Or Rover's."

Ruprecht looked at me like I was the village idiot. "Then whose stomach was it?"

A terrible feeling came over me. I looked down at the raft.

It was only now that I realized that there was something un-raftlike about it.

Rafts are generally made of several logs strapped together and therefore have the texture of tree bark. What we were on was bark-colored, but the texture was more like scales.

(You might be thinking to yourself, *Boy oh boy, Tim isn't very observant. How did he not pick up on this earlier?* Well, keep in mind that I'm not as worldly as you. I had never *seen* a raft before. Or a river, for that matter. These were all very new things to me.)

"I think this raft isn't a raft at all," I said worriedly. "I think it's alive."

Belinda and Nerlim immediately grew frightened. Even Ferkle stopped picking his nose and looked somewhat concerned.

However, Prince Ruprecht laughed at me.

"Alive?" he asked. "How could a raft be alive? It's just an object, you dimwit. See?" With that, he stabbed his sword down into it.

The raft didn't like that at all.

Because I was right. It *wasn't* a raft. Which became evident when it roared angrily. And then did this:

As you can see, we had been riding on the back of a sea serpent . . . or a river serpent . . . or a sea serpent who was on vacation in a river.

Whatever the case, it was a bad mistake.

The serpent bucked wildly, flinging us all high in the

air. And then everyone started plummeting back down toward the water.

Except me. Because I was plummeting straight down toward *this*:

This was not a very good place to be.

I desperately tried to come up with ways to avoid falling straight into the serpent's mouth, but in the brief period of time I was hanging in the air, I only had two ideas:

1) Learn how to fly.

I recognize that this one wasn't really possible. But like I said, I was desperate.

2) Do *this*:

I have to admit, it worked out better than I had hoped.

I don't think the serpent usually consumed people who were wearing armor. (It probably usually ate peasants. Or, if it really was a sea serpent on vacation, it might have normally eaten sailors or pirates.) So I was a lot heavier and harder than it was expecting. I came down like an anvil on its head, knocking it unconscious.

It promptly collapsed in the river, landing with such force that it created a great wave, which caught me and everyone else as we landed and swept us quickly downstream.

Which was where things got *really* dangerous.

CHAPTER ELEVEN

Why I Really Really *Really* Don't Like Traveling on Rivers

While the upper reaches of the river had been nice and calm, we now arrived at a gorge that looked like this:

The great wave pulled us right into a series of rapids and whirlpools. We were all tossed, turned, spun, tumbled, flung, thrashed, smashed, swirled, and whirled about. We banged off rocks, slammed into the sides of the canyon, and clanged into one another.

And then we went over a waterfall.

It wasn't enormous, but it was still big enough to scare me silly. We shot over the lip and dropped down into the churning, foaming rapids at the base. Finally, we were spit out into the river, which became nice and calm again.

Which was the worst part of all.

I know that doesn't seem right. So let me explain:

Armor is heavy.

Heavy things sink.

Up until this point, the water had been moving so fast that we hadn't been given a chance to sink, but now that the water was much calmer, we stopped moving forward . . . and started moving downward.

I realized this was about to happen and yelled to my fellow knights, "Take off your armor as fast as you can!"

The others realized what I meant and scrambled to do this. Even Ferkle. Although Ferkle didn't need to, because somehow, the river had tossed him onto the shore. But, being the village idiot, he still took off his armor to keep himself from drowning.

Ruprecht did not heed my advice. Instead, he got

annoyed. "I'm not taking off my armor!" he yelled. "This was a present to me from my parents! It's the finest armor available in the entire world, and I'm not about to let it sink to the glub glub glub burble burble glub!" (That last bit was the sound of him getting sucked under.)

I managed to get the last of my armor off before getting dragged down for good. As the heavy metal pieces sank to the bottom of the river, I returned to the surface and gasped for air. Belinda and Nerlim and the horses were all gasping beside me.

Rover was just fine, because, being a fr-dog, he could swim.

Ruprecht was drowning.

I dove down again. Ruprecht was standing on the bottom of the river in his armor. The look on his face was slowly shifting from stubborn determination to protect his armor to the realization that he had made a very bad decision. He started struggling to get out of his armor, pulling off the various pieces, but he wasn't quite fast enough.

Luckily, I was there to help him. And so was Belinda. We managed to pry off the last of Ruprecht's armor, then pulled him back up to the surface, getting him there right before he blacked out.

Ruprecht sucked in great big gulps of air as we swam to shore with him.

Then we flopped down on the muddy bank, exhausted from our ordeal and our multiple brushes with death. Nerlim was already lying there in the mud, looking wiped out. Ferkle was busily putting mud in his pants, but a bit more slowly than usual. The horses clambered out of the water close by.

"To heck with this quest," Ruprecht's horse said. "I quit."

"Me too," said Nerlim's horse.

"So do I," Belinda's horse said. "This mission is way too dangerous."

"Let's go home," mine said.

"Wait one second," Ruprecht said to the horses. "You can talk???"

"Of course we can talk," his horse replied. "*All* horses can."

"Why didn't you ever say anything before?" Ruprecht asked.

"You never asked me anything before, did you?" his horse shot back, sounding a little offended. "Did you ever ask how my day was? Or if my saddle was a little too tight? Or if *I* thought it would be a good idea to get on a random raft in the middle of the River of Doom? No! You did not! You just acted like I was some sort of pack animal!"

"Er . . . ," Nerlim said. "But you *are* a pack animal."

"A pack animal with *feelings*!" Ruprecht's horse sniffed. "And I've had enough! So long!" He stormed off.

"See ya!" Nerlim's horse said, and he stormed off too.

"Bye-bye!" Belinda's horse said, following the others.

"*Ciao,*" my horse said. Apparently he was bilingual. He pranced away angrily.

"I like sugar!" Ferkle's mule said. He didn't seem to have been following the conversation.

"Don't mind him," Nerlim's horse called back to us. "He's the stable idiot."

Ruprecht looked after the horses helplessly. "Wait!" he called out. "Charger, don't go. . . ."

His horse glanced back. "My name is not Charger!" he snapped. "It is Fiddlesticks Rumproast the Fourth! Not that you ever bothered to find out!" With that, he galloped away with the other horses, leaving us behind.

Ruprecht stared after them for a bit, then wheeled on Belinda and me. "Well now look what you've gotten us into!" he exclaimed. "You must be the worst group of knights of all time!"

This outburst caught me completely by surprise. To be honest, it really hurt my feelings. I wanted to tell Ruprecht this, but I didn't know how. After all, he was the prince, and I was only a peasant, and it didn't seem like I could say anything to him.

However, Belinda had no such concerns. She was furious. "You think *we're* bad?" she exploded. "If it wasn't for us, you'd be dead at the bottom of the river right now!"

"Only because you got me tossed into this river in the first place!" Ruprecht replied.

"*You* were the one who made us get onto a sea serpent!" Belinda shouted. "*You* were the one who stabbed it! And *you* were the bonehead who refused to take off his armor!"

Ruprecht gasped. "How dare you insult me! I am Prince Ruprecht the Great and Mighty and Hircine!" ("Hircine" means "having a strong, goatish smell." It is very likely that Ruprecht did not know this and misspoke here.) Although he was yelling at us, I got the sense that, deep down inside, he was really worried and scared. Unfortunately, instead of admitting those emotions, he was being awfully mean to us. "I should arrest you right

here, march you back to the village, and have you thrown into the dungeon for your bad attitude!"

"I'd like to see you try!" Belinda said.

Ruprecht was about to respond to this, but Nerlim rushed over, looking very worried, and said, "A word with you, Your Excellency?" He then yanked Ruprecht into a clump of trees. "You need to get a grip on yourself," he hissed.

"But this quest is a disaster!" Ruprecht whined. "Every kingdom in the realm thinks I'm going to rescue the princess! Do you realize what will happen if I don't? Everyone will think I'm a failure!"

"That won't happen," Nerlim assured him, and then said some other things, although I couldn't make them out, because they had moved deeper into the forest.

I turned to Belinda. "What were you thinking just now? You can't speak to the prince like that!"

"Did you hear how he spoke to *us*?! He insulted us for no good reason—and right after we saved his life!"

"Maybe it *was* our fault that he nearly drowned," I said. "If I had tried to help him with his armor first instead of mine . . ."

"Then you'd both have drowned. Don't make excuses for him, Tim. He's not excellent at all. He's selfish and rude and unpleasant. Maybe we should do what our horses did and head home."

"But what about Princess Grace?" I asked.

Belinda didn't have an answer to that. "Oh. I forgot about the princess."

Nerlim and Ruprecht emerged from the trees again. Nerlim was smiling at us. Ruprecht still looked pouty.

"The prince thinks he may have spoken in haste," Nerlim said. "He was out of sorts after nearly drowning and might have turned his anger toward you, rather than the sea serpent, which is who he was *really* angry at. In truth, he thinks that you are all good and noble knights, and he would like to apologize for his behavior and ask you to continue with him on his quest to save the princess. Isn't that right, Ruprecht?"

"Yes," Ruprecht said, although it sounded as though it pained him to do so. He then smiled at us. It did not seem to be a very genuine smile. "That is right."

"Well, that's settled!" Nerlim said. "Why don't we make

camp here and have a nice meal? Oh look! Ferkle seems to have a fish in his pants!"

Nerlim yanked the fish out. "Why don't I fry this over a campfire, and then we can all get a good night's rest and be raring to go in the morning?"

"That sounds like a good idea," I said. I was hungry and exhausted and eager to have a meal that wasn't gruel for the first time in my life.

Belinda reluctantly agreed.

Ferkle looked in his pants to see what else might be in there.

"Great!" Nerlim said. "I'll bet that, after a good meal and some shut-eye, we'll have a much better day tomorrow!"

I nodded enthusiastically, liking the sound of this.

I couldn't imagine that the next day could possibly be worse.

But it was.

CHAPTER TWELVE

What We Talked about That Night

Some time later, after our bellies were full of fish and our clothes were somewhat dry from the fire, Belinda, Nerlim, and I found ourselves lying on the ground, looking up at the stars.

Ruprecht was already asleep, snoring loudly.

Ferkle was looking for a nice, hard rock to use as a pillow.

Rover was curled up at my feet.

Besides our campfire, there was no other light. The sky above us was inky dark and full of tiny little pricks of twinkly lights.

"Nerlim," Belinda said, "when we were facing the sea serpent—or getting swept through the rapids—or sinking into the river—why didn't you just do some magic and save all of us?"

"Er . . . magic?" Nerlim asked.

"Yes," Belinda said. "Being a wizard, you *can* do magic, right? So why didn't you turn the sea serpent into something less dangerous, like a kitten? Or make us levitate so that we didn't go over the waterfall?"

"Well . . . ," Nerlim said. "There are many different kinds of magic. The type you are describing there is one sort. Whereas my magic is of a different sort."

"What sort of magic can you do?" I asked.

"Card tricks, mostly. I can also juggle."

Belinda sat up and narrowed her eyes. "Card tricks? Those aren't magic! They're just fakery!"

"They're very good card tricks," Nerlim said weakly. Then he pulled a deck of damp cards from his robe and fanned them out. "I'll show you. Pick a card, any card. . . ."

I interrupted him. "How did you ever get to be the wizard to the royal family if you can't do *real* magic?"

"Ah!" Nerlim said. "Well . . . you see . . . er . . . um . . . the fact of the matter is that . . . er . . ."

"They don't know you can't do magic, do they?" Belinda asked.

"No," Nerlim admitted, looking down at the ground. "They don't."

"How is that possible?" I asked.

"The king and queen are very gullible," Nerlim said, his gaze lifting up to meet mine and then moving over to Belinda. "So I . . . well . . . I kind of fooled them into thinking I would be a good wizard."

"Why?" I asked.

"It was that or be a peasant," Nerlim replied. "And I really hated peasanting. So I learned a few magic tricks and found a way to change my station in life." He paused, looking into the fire. "I guess that might sound kind of ridiculous."

"No," I said. "I understand not wanting to be a peasant really well."

"Still," Belinda said, "it doesn't seem right that you've been lying to everyone all along."

"But lying about being a boy to become a knight is all right?" Nerlim asked.

Belinda's eyes went wide. "Urk," she said. "How did you know?"

"I overheard you both in town while you were on the way to the tryouts."

Belinda and I both winced at our mistake.

"Oops," I said.

"And you let me be a knight anyway?" Belinda asked, surprised.

"I've always felt the rule that only men should be knights was wrongheaded," Nerlim told her. "It seems to me that if a woman is just as capable as a man, then she should have the same opportunities a man does."

"Really?" Belinda said, sounding pleased by Nerlim's attitude.

"Yes. And also, we needed as many knights as we could get, and you were the only ones who showed up to the tryouts."

"Ah," Belinda said, not sounding quite so pleased anymore.

"However, the prince isn't nearly as open-minded as I am where girls are concerned," Nerlim warned. "So let's make a deal. If you don't tell him that I'm a fraud, I won't tell him you're a girl."

"Okay," Belinda agreed.

Nerlim smiled. "Good. Now, we have a big day tomorrow. Let's get some sleep." He found a wad of moss to use as a pillow and stretched out by the fire.

Belinda didn't make any move to go to sleep, though. She kept staring into the flames. "Lying about being a wizard seems worse than lying about being a girl," she said quietly. "He could be a better wizard if he wanted to. But I can't do anything about being a girl. It's not fair that I can't be a knight, just because of how I was born."

"I know," I agreed.

"I *wish* I could have been happy being a housewife or a witch," Belinda said. "But I wouldn't be. And I can't change who I am."

"I can't either," I said. "Being a knight is *scary*. But I wouldn't give it up to become a peasant again."

"Me neither," Belinda agreed. "Thank goodness Rover came along, though."

"Yeah," I agreed, then looked at my fr-dog. "Do you think life would be easier if we were dogs? Or frogs? Or fr-dogs? Do you think Rover ever wishes he could be something else?"

"Beats me," Belinda said. "I wonder what he's thinking right now."

"I guess we'll never know," I said.

What Rover Was Actually Thinking

Dum de dum de dum de doo. Doo be doo be doo. Dum dum dum dum. Doo be doo. Dum de dum de dum de doo. Doo be doo be doo. Dum dum dum dum. Doo be doo. Dum de dum de dum de doo.

Doo be doo be doo. Dum dum dum dum. Doo be doo. Dum de dum de dum de doo. Doo be doo be doo. Dum dum dum dum. Doo be doo. FOOD! Dum de dum de dum de doo. Doo be doo

be doo. Dum dum dum dum. Doo be doo. Dum de dum de dum de doo. Doo be doo be doo. Dum dum dum dum. Doo be doo. Dum de dum de dum de doo. Doo be doo be doo. Dum dum dum dum. Doo be doo. Dum de dum de dum de doo. Doo be doo be doo. Dum dum dum dum. Doo be doo. Dum de dum de dum de doo. Doo be doo be doo. Dum dum dum dum. Doo be doo. FOOD! Yum yum yum! Dum de dum de dum de doo. Doo be doo be doo. Dum dum dum dum. Doo be doo. Dum de dum de dum de doo. Doo be doo be doo. Dum dum dum dum. Doo be doo. Dum de dum de dum de doo. Doo be doo be doo. Dum dum dum dum. Doo be doo. Dum de dum de dum de doo. Doo be doo be doo. Dum dum dum dum. Doo be doo. ZZZZZZZZZZZ.

CHAPTER THIRTEEN

What Horrible Trouble We Ran into the Next Day

Early the next morning, shortly after breakfast, we found ourselves trapped on a troll bridge over the Chasm of Doom.

No, not a TOLL bridge. A toll bridge looks like this:

A toll bridge is a bridge where a monetary charge is required to pass from one side to the other.

Meanwhile, a TROLL bridge looks like this:

A troll bridge is a bridge infested with trolls that generally trap the travelers in the middle with the intent to eat them. The travelers then have a choice: 1) Get eaten. 2) Jump from the bridge, then fall to a miserable, painful death at the bottom of the chasm, followed by getting eaten anyhow.

Needless to say, it is not much fun to find yourself on a troll bridge.

Toll bridges might not be much fun either, but still, the next time you find yourself stuck in a line of cars to pay a few bucks, and your parents are griping about the traffic and the cost and how much they hate commuting, feel free to remind them that things could be a *lot* worse.

For example: we were trapped on a poorly built bridge over a vertiginous ⟨ IQ BOOSTER! ⟩ ravine, surrounded by homicidal ⟨ IQ BOOSTER! ⟩ trolls. ("Vertiginous" means "causing unease, usually by being very high and steep," while "homicidal" means "really, really vicious." Just because your life is about to end doesn't mean you can't build up your vocabulary.) Also, we didn't have any armor or weapons, because they had all sunk to the bottom of the river, and our horses had fled, because they were quitters.

(Here's how a horse would have come in handy in this situation: horses are a lot bigger than humans, so if the trolls had eaten them first, then maybe they would have been too full to eat *us*. I know that there are lots of animal-rights groups that frown on the idea of feeding horses to trolls, but trust me, if you have to make a choice between you or your horse getting eaten, it's not too difficult.)

So, we were in quite a predicament. ⟨YET ANOTHER IQ BOOSTER!⟩ (A predicament is a difficult, unpleasant or embarrassing situation. If you happen to be reading this book in class instead of paying attention to your lessons and then laugh loudly at one of the many hilarious jokes, alerting your teacher to what you are doing, then you might find yourself in quite a predicament.)

"Hey there," the slightly uglier troll said cheerfully. "My name is Argleblarrrrgh. And my friend on the other side of the ravine is Pete. We'll be consuming you for breakfast this morning."

"Would you mind if I eat the three humans closest to me?" Pete asked Argleblarrrrgh. "And you take the other two and the giant frog. You know how frogs give me gas."

"Do I ever," said Argleblarrrrgh.

"No one will be eating anyone today!" Prince Ruprecht shouted with surprising force. "You both have made a terrible mistake. Because this man here is the most masterful wizard in all the land!" He pointed directly at Nerlim.

Nerlim gulped audibly.

"This is Nerlim the Great and Powerful!" Ruprecht proclaimed. "And if you so much as take one step toward us, he will blast you with the most awesome magic known to man and turn you both into newts!"

Nerlim grew increasingly nervous.

Ruprecht continued yelling at the trolls. "And then, after that, he will blast you with lightning bolts of flame and fry you into crispy critters!"

Nerlim now looked like he might throw up.

"And after that," Ruprecht continued, "he'll make you explode into smithereens! And then he'll turn each one of those smithereens into a teensy newt and start the whole process over again!"

Argleblarrrrgh gave Nerlim a skeptical look. "Really? He doesn't look that powerful to *me*."

"Just test him!" Ruprecht challenged.

Nerlim shot Belinda and me a glance that meant *Get me out of this.*

Argleblarrrrgh and Pete looked at each other over the Chasm of Doom. "I think they're bluffing," Argleblarrrrgh said. "How about you?"

"Yeah," Pete said. "I think they're bluffing too."

Both of them started coming for us.

Ruprecht looked at Nerlim expectantly. "Well?" he said. "Let them have it!"

Nerlim smiled weakly in return.

Pete was just about to grab Belinda. There was nowhere for her to run.

"Wait!" I yelled as loudly and forcefully as I could.

Both trolls froze mid-grab.

Which gave me half of a moment to come up with a plan. And I actually did.

"We're not bluffing!" I announced. Then I pointed to Rover. "See this giant frog here? That used to be our lead knight! But he stepped on Nerlim's toe yesterday, so Nerlim did this to him!"

The trolls looked at Rover curiously. "Really?" Pete asked.

"Yes!" I said. "Do you honestly think we'd be traveling with a giant frog otherwise?"

"Hmmm," Argleblarrrrgh said thoughtfully. "That *did* seem odd to me."

"But," Pete added cautiously, "it's not like we saw

that happen. So we don't have any proof."

"You want proof?" I asked. "I'll tell you what. Nerlim could turn one of you into a really enormous frog, and then the other one would see that we're not joking around. So, which of you should Nerlim zap?"

Argleblarrrrgh and Pete immediately pointed at each other. "Him," both said at once.

And then each of them grew upset that the other had done this. "How dare you sacrifice me!" they yelled at each other.

"*I* shouldn't get turned into a frog!" Argleblarrrrgh argued. "I'm the brains of this operation!"

"*I'm* the brains!" Pete yelled. "You're an idiot!"

"Well you're ugly!" Argleblarrrrgh yelled back.

I had never encountered a troll before, but I had always heard that they had very short tempers. Thankfully, this proved to be the case. In a matter of moments, Argleblarrrrgh and Pete were screaming at each other.

"You're the ugly one!"

"Well you're even uglier!"

"You're a loser!"

"You stink!"

"I'm gonna make you eat those words!"

"I'd like to see you try!"

Then Argleblarrrrgh leapt across the Chasm of Doom and clubbed Pete on the head. Pete clubbed him right back. And then they started pounding, kicking, strangling, throttling, gouging, and pummeling each other.

They fought so hard that the mountains shook.

While they were distracted trying to kill each other, we raced across the bridge and hurried up the narrow trail on the other side.

"That was some good thinking back there," Belinda told me.

"Humph," Ruprecht scoffed. "We didn't *need* good thinking. Nerlim was just about to turn them into newts before you interrupted. Now they're still alive, and we're going to have to face them on the way back."

From behind us came the distinct sound of two angry trolls knocking each other into a very steep chasm and then wailing in fear and then splatting at the bottom.

"Then again, maybe we won't," I said.

"Humph," Ruprecht scoffed again. Then he turned to Nerlim. "If we run into trouble with this stinx, don't hesitate to use your magic on it. Just turn it into a newt or a slug or a potato or something. Got it?"

"Er . . . yes, of course," Nerlim agreed.

"Good," Ruprecht said. "The next part of this quest won't be any trouble at all."

Which, of course, was totally wrong.

CHAPTER FOURTEEN

What We Found in the Lair of the Stinx

The stinx's lair wasn't hard to find. All we had to do was follow the smell.

Not far beyond the Chasm of Doom, things began to get a bit rank. Then they got musty. And then they got fetid, pungent, acrid, putrid, noxious, malodorous (you remember that word, right?)—until eventually, we arrived at the lair at the top of the mountain, where the smell could only be described as HOLY COW THIS IS THE MOST HORRIBLE, DISGUSTING, AWFUL STENCH I HAVE EVER ENCOUNTERED ON EARTH.

We all had to jam bits of cloth up our noses so that we didn't get woozy from the smell.

For once, luck appeared
to be on our side. The
stinx wasn't at home. The
cave still *smelled* terrible,
though, and it was littered
with gnawed bones.

"Bere do you dink it
ibbs?" Belinda asked.
(Her words sounded
funny because of the cloth
jammed up her nose.)

"Brobably terrorbizing a billage," Ruprecht said.
(His words also sounded funny because of the cloth
jammed up his nose.) "Does anyone see Brincess Brace?"

Ferkle suddenly let out a gasp of surprise, pointed
across the room, and promptly passed out. (He had fool-
ishly put the bits of cloth in his ears and the smell had
overwhelmed him.)

We all looked to where he had pointed. Sure enough,
we could see the distant form of Princess Grace far across
the cave.

"Fear not, fair maiden!" Prince Ruprecht yelled at the top of his lungs. (Although it came out as "Beer not, bear baitin!") "I'll save you!" He dashed across the cave, swept the princess up in his arms and gazed adoringly into her eyes.

And then her head fell off.

This was quite a shock for Prince Ruprecht. He shrieked and promptly passed out as well.

Belinda, Nerlim, and I hurried over. (Although, I have to admit, I might not have hurried quite as much as the others, because I was really in no rush to see a headless princess.)

Rover started gnawing on one of the bones.

Belinda, Nerlim, and I steeled ourselves for the sight of some disgusting carnage, but instead found this:

"It's a *doll*," I observed.

"Then bear is the brincess?" Nerlim asked.

"Hi there," Princess Grace said, stepping out of the shadows.

"AAAAAAAAUUUUUGGGGGGHHHHHHHH!" Belinda, Nerlim, and I screamed, because we were really not expecting this.

"Oh sorry," Grace said. "I didn't mean to scare you." (She was speaking totally normally, because she did not have bits of cloth jammed into her nostrils. Also, she was wearing a burlap sack, because her dress was on the doll.)

We finally managed to recover our breath enough to pepper her with questions.

"Bar you bokay?" Nerlim asked.

"Bhat is bappening beer?" Belinda asked.

"Bye don't you have bits of bloth buffed bup your bose?" I asked.

"I'm fine," the princess replied. "Turns out, the stinx didn't actually want to steal *me*. It only wanted a dress for its doll. I just happened to be wearing the one it liked best at the time. And I *did* have bits of cloth jammed up my nose for a while, but it was annoying. To be honest, you get used to the stench after a day or so."

Nerlim, Belinda, and I had plenty of follow-up questions, mostly about the stinx having a doll, but before we could ask them, a shadow fell over all of us.

Our luck seemed to have run out.

The stinx was home.

CHAPTER FIFTEEN

What I Learned about the Stinx

Belinda, Nerlim, and I turned around slowly, expecting to find ourselves face-to-face with the most vicious, terrifying, ill-tempered beast imaginable.

Instead, we found this:

"Awwwwww!" Belinda exclaimed. "It's a baby!!!!"

"And it's adorable!!!!" Nerlim added.

(You may have noticed I dropped the weird spellings of our words due to our plugged-up noses. I was worried it would get difficult to read. And the joke had already gone on long enough. Rest assured, our noses were still plugged, and we sounded ridiculous.)

The stinx meowed in a way that was absolutely enchanting from both of its heads at once. Then it gamboled back toward what it had brought to the lair from its travels that day: a dollhouse.

Although it wasn't *exactly* a dollhouse. It was a *house*. The little stinx had ripped the entire thing out of the ground and flown it back to its lair. (Luckily, there were no peasants in it, although I suspected that the owners were probably going to be quite peeved when they returned home to find their house wasn't there anymore.)

The stinx gripped it in its claws (which were razor sharp, but still somehow precious), then flapped it over to where the makeshift doll in Princess Grace's dress lay. It set the house down, grabbed the doll to put it in the house, then noticed the head was missing . . .

And started to cry.

"Ohhh!" Princess Grace gasped. "Don't worry, Fluffy!" She raced over to help set the pumpkin back in place on the doll's neck. "I'll have this fixed in a jiffy!"

"So . . . ," I said, "the stinx didn't capture you for any evil purpose?"

"Oh no!" Grace said. "Fluffy here is a sweetheart! It was all just an accident!"

"But her parents aren't so sweet, right?" Nerlim asked. "They're evil, vicious, and bloodthirsty beasts."

"Not at all," Grace said. "In fact, they have been quite lovely to me."

"But I had always heard that stinxes were awful, terrible, horrendous creatures," Belinda said.

"So had I," Grace replied. "I guess you can't believe everything that you hear."

Nerlim frowned at this, which seemed a strange reaction to me.

But at the moment, I was more focused on the princess. "So you weren't being held prisoner here?" I asked her.

"No."

"And you could have left at any time?"

"I suppose."

"So why didn't you?"

Princess Grace paused to think about this, as though the idea of leaving had never even occurred to her. "That wouldn't be right, would it?"

"What do you mean?" Belinda asked.

"Well, I'm a princess, and when a princess gets into trouble, she's not supposed to just rescue herself. She's supposed to wait for a brave and handsome prince to come along and rescue her—and once he does, they look into each other's eyes and fall madly in love—and probably sing a delightful song about it." She looked all of us over. "So then, which of you is the prince?" She gave Nerlim a worried glance. "It's not *you*, is it?"

"No," Nerlim said.

Princess Grace heaved a sigh of relief.

"The prince is right there, at your feet," Nerlim told her, looking slightly offended. "He passed out a little while ago."

Princess Grace looked down and noticed Ruprecht sprawled on the ground. "Oh," she said. "He seems quite handsome. Although it's a bit hard to tell because his face is smushed into the floor." She finally got the pumpkin head onto the doll's body properly. "There you go, Fluffster," she told the young stinx. "Good as new!"

The little stinx mewled with joy and started playing with its doll.

"Let me get this straight," Belinda said. "You *could* have rescued yourself at any time, but you stayed because society has taught you that you had to wait for a man to come and save you?"

"Yes!" Princess Grace said brightly. "And then we will get married and have the most beautiful wedding in history!"

"You have to be kidding me," Belinda said. "You'd fall in love with a man just because he rescued you?"

"Er . . . ," Grace said, pausing to think about this. "How else would I fall in love with someone?"

"Maybe by meeting them and getting to know them?" Belinda suggested. "A woman shouldn't love a man only because he did something for her. She should love him for being a good person with strong morals and similar interests and hobbies. And a sense of humor is also a plus."

"Hmmm," Grace said thoughtfully. "I suppose that makes sense."

"And also," Belinda went on, "this whole idea that you shouldn't be able to rescue yourself because you're a woman is garbage. Women can do anything that men can."

"Wow," Grace said. "You have some very radical ideas. But I kind of like them."

"Well *I* don't!" Prince Ruprecht exclaimed. It turned out he had regained consciousness—and was now quite angry. He leapt to his feet and told Princess Grace, "I am the Most Excellent and Brave Prince Ruprecht, and I have saved you from the vile stinx! It is only right for you to fall madly in love with me!"

"But you *didn't* save me from the stinx," Princess Grace reminded him. "I was never really in danger—and you've been passed out the whole time."

"That's *your* story," Ruprecht said. "But the people of our kingdoms will believe *mine* instead. After all, you're only a woman, while I am a man!"

"But we're men too," I said, pointing to myself and Nerlim and Belinda (which was a lie, but Ruprecht didn't know that). "And we know the truth."

"Good point," Ruprecht said. "We'll have to do something about that."

He then pulled out a fish that he'd had hidden in his breeches and pointed it menacingly at me.

"Er . . . ," I said, confused. "What are you doing?"

"Oh. This was supposed to be a knife," Ruprecht said, looking quite embarrassed. "I was going to kill you with it to protect my secret, but this dumb fish must have ended up in my scabbard when we were in the River of Doom. I *thought* my knife felt slimier than usual."

"That will still be of service," Nerlim noted. "What you have there is a Dastardly Deathfish. It has razor-sharp teeth and enough venom in its spines to kill a dragon. Just shake it a little."

Curious, Prince Ruprecht shook the fish. To our surprise, lots of very scary-looking spines popped out of it.

"Hey!" Ruprecht exclaimed, sounding pleasantly surprised. "Look at that! This is *way* better than a knife. I can't believe I've been carrying this thing in my breeches all day."

I wheeled on Nerlim, annoyed that he'd helped Prince Ruprecht, only to discover that he had an actual knife in his hands—and it was pointed at Belinda.

Belinda and I did not have knives. Or Dastardly Deathfish. Or any sort of weapons at all. And we were backed up against the wall of the cave with nowhere to run. So our chances of survival were suddenly infinitesimal.

("Infinitesimal" means "really, really small." Basically, our gooses were cooked.)

CHAPTER SIXTEEN

Why We Were Betrayed

"Hold on," I said nervously. "You're really going to kill us just to keep it a secret that you didn't rescue the princess?"

"Yes," Ruprecht said. "In fact, that was our plan all along: find some dummies to do the dirty work for us, then get rid of them so that they couldn't tell everyone the truth."

Belinda turned to Nerlim, surprised. "You were in on this?"

"It was *my* idea," Nerlim said, flashing an evil grin. "You see, the reputation of a prince means a great deal. We can't have everyone knowing he's a lily-livered coward who runs from the slightest sign of danger. Then he'd be the laughingstock of all the other kingdoms."

"But I saved your life!" I reminded the prince. "You'd have drowned if it wasn't for me! And you're still going to kill me?"

"Yes," Ruprecht replied. "You're only a peasant, after all. No one will even miss you. Whereas *I* am important! I am the Most Excellent and Brave Prince Ruprecht!"

"But that's a lie!" Belinda cried.

"And it's my job to make sure everyone believes it," Nerlim said. "Which may be morally questionable, but is still far better than peasanting."

Ruprecht advanced on us with his Dastardly Deathfish, which hissed in a very menacing manner and gnashed its disturbingly sharp teeth. But while the fish looked extremely dangerous, Ruprecht himself looked rather weaselly. "I know being a prince must seem awfully easy to you peasants," he said. "But in truth, it's a very stressful job. There's a tremendous amount of pressure to project the right image. When a princess gets captured, you can't just stay at home, playing Parcheesi. You have to risk life and limb to go rescue her. Or, at least, trick someone else into doing that for you. If it's any consolation, you have served me well. I will never forget the great sacrifices the two of you made to help me rescue my fair and lovely bride-to-be. . . ."

"Um . . . ," Princess Grace said. "I haven't agreed to marry you yet."

"But you will, of course," Ruprecht replied. "Because you are a silly, helpless princess, and I am the prince who rescued you from a terrible fate. Plus, I am also devastatingly handsome. I mean, who else are you going to marry? One of these losers? They're just peasants!"

He said the word "peasants" with disgust, in the same way that some people would say "head lice" or "intestinal parasites" or "lawyers." It made me very upset.

"We're not peasants anymore," I said angrily. "We're *knights*."

"Only because I *said* you were knights," Ruprecht sneered. "The truth is, you're nothing. I'm the prince and you're my subjects, which means that I will always be superior to you. I could force you to be my royal-buttocks wipers if I wanted to, and you'd have to do it. Because life is unfair and there's nothing you can do about it." He threw his head back and laughed at us mockingly. "Ha-ha-ha-ha-ha-ha! Ho-ho-ho-ho-ho! Hee-hee-hee-hee . . . UNNNGGHHHH."

Prince Ruprecht didn't get to finish laughing, because Princess Grace whacked him on the head with one of the many bones that were lying about.

And then, when Nerlim turned to see what had happened, she whacked him, too.

Which left both of our attackers out cold on the floor of the cave with Princess Grace standing over them, looking quite proud of herself.

"There's no way I'm marrying that guy," she said, pointing to Ruprecht's prone body. "He's a jerk."

"Thanks," I said. "I can't believe we came all the way to rescue you—and you ended up rescuing *us*."

"That's what you call irony," Princess Grace said. "Although, I do appreciate all the effort you put into it. I saw you face those trolls down at the Chasm of Doom."

"You did?" I asked, surprised.

"In case you haven't noticed, there's not much to do in this cave," Princess Grace replied. "Waiting for a prince to come and rescue you is really boring. So I was keeping an eye on the route up here. You both handled yourselves so gallantly with the trolls, I thought that perhaps one of *you* was the prince. Plus, you also had to get through the Forest of Doom and across the River of Doom, and I'm guessing this spineless chicken was no help at all." She pointed dismissively at Ruprecht. "I mean, he passed out at the sight of a headless doll."

"You're right," Belinda agreed. "He didn't do diddly-squat."

Princess Grace looked to her thankfully. "I don't think I would have ever thought to stand up for myself if it wasn't for you. I owe you for that. And despite the terrible things that nasty Prince Ruprecht said about you, you are both obviously very brave and gallant young knights."

"We *were*," Belinda said. She looked at the prone bodies of Ruprecht and Nerlim. "I don't think these guys are going to let us keep our jobs."

"No," I said sadly. Even though being a knight had been one terrifying ordeal after another, it had also been the most exciting part of my life. "I guess we're back to being peasants again."

"Not necessarily," Princess Grace said. "I could certainly use some brave and gallant knights to protect me—and advise me on ethical issues as well. Would you be interested?"

Belinda and I shared a look of excitement, then turned back to Princess Grace.

"Of course!" I exclaimed.

"Absolutely!" Belinda chimed in.

Princess Grace smiled at us. "Very good! Then your first mission is helping me return home to my kingdom safely."

"Sounds good!" I said, but then frowned at the thought of what that entailed. "Although, it's going to be quite an arduous ◁ IQ BOOSTER! journey.

"What does 'arduous' mean?" Princess Grace asked, before I could even define it for all of you.

"Difficult and strenuous," I answered. "We will have to pass back over the Chasm of Doom and confront those trolls again, who—if they're still alive—are going to be even angrier at us, and then we'll have to go along the River of Doom and back through the Forest of Doom, too. . . ."

"Actually, I have a suggestion that would allow us to avoid all that trouble," someone said.

The three of us turned around and discovered, to our surprise, that Ferkle was the one who had said it. Not only could he speak, but his tone was educated and thoughtful.

"We could simply have the stinx fly us back home," he went on. "After all, it flew Princess Grace here in the first place. And despite its young age, according to my estimates, it easily has the size and strength to carry the four of us and Rover. In this way, we would avoid all of the various perils and arrive home with considerable expeditiousness." IQ BOOSTER!

("Expeditiousness" means "speed." And I was just as amazed that Ferkle knew that word as you were.)

Belinda and I gaped at him in shock.

"You can *talk*?" I asked.

"You're *smart?*" Belinda exclaimed.

"Uh . . . yes," Ferkle said, looking embarrassed.

"But you're the village idiot!" I said. "You're supposed to be . . . well . . . an idiot."

"Right," Ferkle agreed. "Well, you see, it's all an issue of expectations. My father was the village idiot. And his father was the village idiot before him. And *his* father was the village idiot before that. And *his* father was the village numbskull, which was what they called the job back in those days. So of course, I was expected to be the village idiot. My parents were very upset when I turned out to be smart. But . . . it's the family business, so I had no choice but to go into it. Do any of you have anything weird I could put in my nose, like a turnip?"

I was now stunned on many different levels, and yet, I couldn't deny one thing. "That's a great plan," I said.

"It is!" Belinda agreed.

"I like it," Princess Grace seconded.

"Ribbit," said Rover, who looked up from the bone

he was chewing and wagged the place where his tail had once been.

"Fluffy," Princess Grace said to the little stinx, "would you mind flying us home? You can keep my dress for your doll."

The young stinx looked up from playing and shook both its heads. It was in no hurry to go.

"If you take us, you can keep this prince and this wizard to play with," Ferkle said, pointing to our unconscious enemies.

The little stinx smiled on both faces and nodded both heads excitedly.

So the rest of us clambered up onto its back and went home like this:

CHAPTER SEVENTEEN

How Everything Worked Out

So that's how I became a knight.

And how Belinda became one too.

But not Ferkle. He decided to go back to just being the village idiot, which he considered much less life-threatening. (Which was further proof that he wasn't that dumb after all—although I do think the putting-mud-in-his-pants thing was pretty weird.)

I think my parents might have been kind of proud of me.

Obviously, my first quest didn't go exactly as I had planned, but I learned some things this time around. Most importantly: don't believe everything you hear.

Princes aren't always brave and honorable.

Some wizards can't do any magic at all.

Some beasts aren't nearly as vicious and mean as people say they are.

Princesses don't always need a hero to rescue them—and if they do, they're under no legal obligation to fall in love with that person.

Just because someone is the village idiot doesn't mean they're an idiot. (Although it usually does.)

So if someone tells you something, maybe you ought to investigate whether it's true or not, instead of blindly believing it.

At least, that's what I'm going to do from now on.

I figure it'll help me out on my next adventure—and I'm pretty sure there will be lots more adventures to come.

Because, sadly, in my time, no one really lives Happily Ever After. That's just something storybooks say. In reality, we're merely Happy for the Time Being.

So stay tuned. No matter how fancy those last two words at the end of this sentence, this is not . . .

THE END

Acknowledgments

I have never had an illustrated book before. So the first person I need to extend gratitude ⟨IQ BOOSTER!| to is my incredibly talented illustrator, Stacy Curtis, for bringing my characters and this world to life.

("Gratitude" is the quality of being thankful. What I'm saying here is that, without the help of Stacy—or any of the other people I'm going to list below, this book wouldn't exist. It would just be a jumble of really weird ideas in my brain.)

So . . . more gratitude goes to my incredible team at Simon & Schuster for their support for this project: Justin Chanda, my publisher, gave me the opportunity to write this in the first place and my editor, Krista Vitola, oversaw it. And then there's Lucy Cummins, Kendra Levin, Catherine Laudone, Anne Zafian, Milena Giunco, Beth Parker, Lisa Moraleda, Jenica Nasworthy, Tom Daly, Chrissy Noh, Devin MacDonald, Erin Toller,

Anna Jarzab, Brian Murray, Christina Pecorale, Victor Iannone, Emily Hutton, Emily Ritter, Michelle Leo, and Theresa Pang.

Additional gratitude goes to my amazing fellow writers (and support group): Rose Brock, James Ponti, Sarah Mlynowski, Julie Buxbaum, Christina Soontornvat, Karina Yan Glaser, Max Brallier, and Gordon Korman.

Even more gratitude goes to my interns, Caroline Curran and Paola Camacho, as well as Megan Vicente; Barry and Carole Patmore; Suz, Darragh, and Ciara Howard; and Ronald and Jane Gibbs.

And finally, huge heaps of gratitude are due to my kids, Dashiell and Violet, who make me laugh and smile and burst with happiness every day. I love you both more than words can say.

About the Author and Illustrator

Stuart Gibbs is the *New York Times* bestselling author of *Charlie Thorne and the Last Equation*, *Charlie Thorne and the Lost City*, and the FunJungle, Moon Base Alpha, and Spy School series. He has written screenplays, worked on a whole bunch of animated films, developed TV shows, been a newspaper columnist, and researched capybaras (the world's largest rodents). Stuart lives with his family in Los Angeles. You can learn more about what he's up to at stuartgibbs.com.

Stacy Curtis is an award-winning illustrator, cartoonist, and printmaker. He has illustrated more than thirty-five children's books, including *Karate Kakapo*, which won the National Cartoonists Society's Book Illustration award. Stacy lives in the Chicago area with his wife, daughter, and two dogs.